Mounta

written by Susan Hughes
illustrated by Michael Cashmore-Hingley

1

Matt looked at his watch. He got off his bicycle and paced back and forth impatiently, and then looked at his watch again. "Finally!" he exclaimed as his cousin Emma came hurrying out of the front door.

"Sorry I'm late, Matt," she said.

"You're always late," Matt grumbled. "You're so fussy: worrying about this, worrying about that. Everything always takes so much planning. Come on! Let's go!"

Emma attached two nylon bags over the back wheel of her bike, then opened one of the pouches and then the other. "I just want to be certain we have everything we might need. Just in case..."

"In case what?" Matt complained, hands on hips. "Come on – nothing horrible is going to happen. We're just going biking in the mountains."

"Okay, everything's here, including our lunch," Emma said firmly, snapping closed the bags. "Let's go!"

Matt led the way down the road, with Emma following. It was a sunny early winter Saturday morning with only a touch of chill in the air. It wasn't long before the cousins reached the foot of the mountain.

"Need to check the bags again, worrywart?" Matt teased Emma.

"Very funny," she replied, with a grin, readjusting her helmet and racing after him up the trail.

For several hours, the young teens rode along the path which wove back and forth, up and down, all along the bottom slopes of the mountainside.

10

Then, tired and hungry, Emma saw the grassy clearing that made the perfect picnic spot. "Lunchtime!" she sang out. Matt popped a wheelie, jumped off his bike, and leaned it next to hers.

As the cousins ate, they looked out over the spectacular view. Many leaves had fallen, and the crisp air made the river look a vivid blue.

"That was fun," said Emma. "So, ready to head home?"
Matt laughed. "Emma, it's a perfect day. Let's go higher. We've done this bottom route so many times that it isn't challenging anymore. We could do it in our sleep."

Emma hesitated. "Our parents have always refused whenever we've asked to go higher," she reminded him. "Also the weather report says there might be a storm this afternoon."

"Stop being such a worrywart," Matt laughed at her. "Look at the sunshine! Plus, our parents will never know, and if there's any sign of bad weather we'll head right down."

The cousins argued for a while until finally Emma nervously agreed to the adventure. "But we turn back after an hour," she told Matt. "Right?"

The pair headed off on their bikes. Soon they were both equally excited at tackling the new path, a steep one which would test their endurance and skill.

An hour later, exhausted, they were approaching the mountain top when suddenly the storm struck. High winds, snow, dropping temperatures ... "What should we do?" called Matt, with a tremor in his voice. "I can hardly see a thing! It's impossible to tell which way to go!" "Me too," said Emma. "But don't worry, we're going to be fine." She reached into one of the bags and pulled out a compass and a flashlight. "We need to find shelter, so stay calm and follow me."

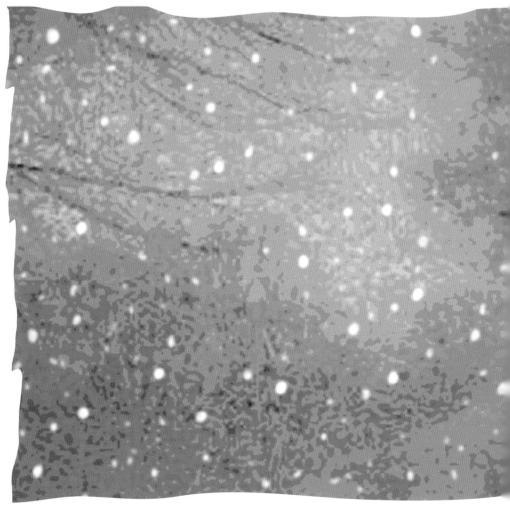

Carefully Emma led the way down the path and back to the tree line. But abruptly the snow turned to rain, and they were now both cold and wet.

Emma searched through the bag again: "First aid kit, whistle, repair kit, pump, water, snacks, flares..." Then she announced, "Here it is! A thermal blanket to keep us warm."

Soon she and Matt were snuggled side by side with the emergency blanket around them.

Then, as suddenly as it had come, the storm vanished. The sun broke through the clouds, the leaves glistened, the wind dropped, and the temperature began to climb.

"Thank goodness!" said Matt, jumping up. "Okay, let's go! We've got to ride down and get home before our parents start wondering where we are!"

But Emma just stood there looking at him, hands on her hips, waiting.